PIP AND KIP

All inquiries should be addressed to:
Barron's Educational Series, Inc.
250 Wireless Boulevard
Hauppauge, NY 11788

International Standard Book No. 0-8120-1454-5

Library of Congress Catalog Card No. 92-29864

Library of Congress Cataloging-in-Publication Data

Foster, Kelli C.
    Kip and Pip/by Foster & Erickson; illustrations by Kerri Gifford.
    p. cm.—(Get ready—get set—read!)
    Summary: As monkey gymnast Pip flips, ostrich spectator Kip trips, thereby getting into the act.
    ISBN 0-8120-1454-5
    (1. Monkeys—Fiction.   2. Ostriches—Fiction.   3. Gymnastics—Fiction.   4. Stories in rhyme.)
I. Erickson, Gina Clegg. II. Gifford, Kerri, ill. III. Title. IV. Series: Erickson, Gina Clegg. Get ready—get set—read!
PZ8.3.F813Ki   1993
(E)—dc20   92-29864
                                                        CIP
                                                        AC

PRINTED IN CHINA
19 18 17 16 15 14 13

GET READY...GET SET...READ!

PIP AND KIP

by
Foster & Erickson

Illustrations by
Kerri Gifford

BARRON'S

Hip-Hip for Pip!

Kip likes to see Pip
zip, skip, and flip.

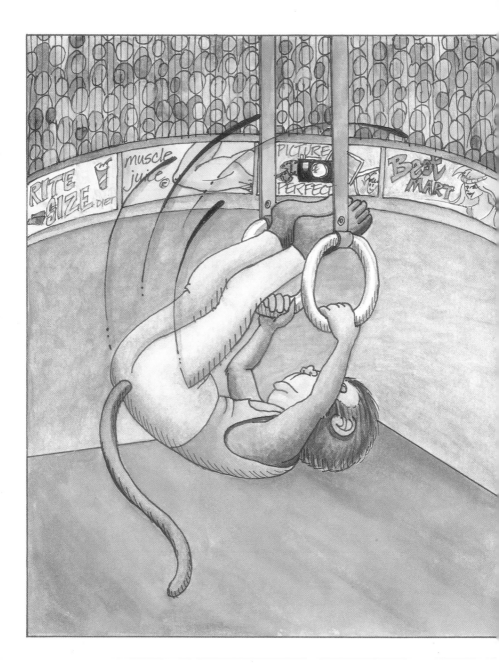

Pip grips and flips.

Kip grips and rips.

Pip dips.

Kip dips and sips.

Hip-hip for Pip!

Oh no! Kip's drink tips.

Pip zips, skips, and flips.

Kip zips, skips, and...

...trips.

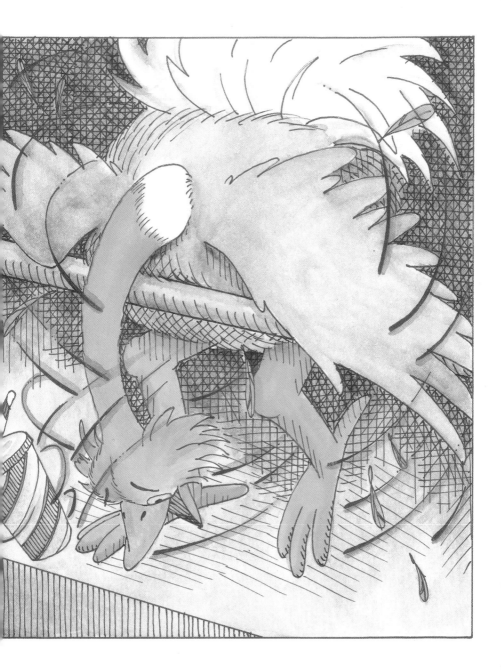

He whips and dips.

He flips and flips.

Kip slips, and then he grips.

Hip-hip-hip for Pip and Kip.

The End

The IP Word Family

dips	sips
flip	skip
flips	skips
grips	slips
hip-hip	tips
Kip	trips
Kip's	whips
Pip	zip
rips	zips

Sight Words

he
oh
no
to
and
for
see
then
drink
likes

Dear Parents and Educators:

Welcome to *Get Ready...Get Set...Read!*

We've created these books to introduce children to the magic of reading.

Each story in the series is built around one or two word families. For example, *A Mop for Pop* uses the OP word family. Letters and letter blends are added to OP to form words such as TOP, LOP, and STOP. As you can see, once children are able to read OP, it is a simple task for them to read the entire word family. In addition to word families, we have used a limited number of "sight words." These are words found to occur with high frequency in the books your child will soon be reading. Being able to identify sight words greatly increases reading skill.

You might find the steps outlined on the facing page useful in guiding your work with your beginning reader.

We had great fun creating these books, and great pleasure sharing them with our children. We hope *Get Ready...Get Set...Read!* helps make this first step in reading fun for you and your new reader.

Kelli C. Foster, PhD
Educational Psychologist

Gina Clegg Erickson, MA
Reading Specialist

Guidelines for Using *Get Ready...Get Set...Read!*

Step 1.   Read the story to your child.

Step 2.   Have your child read the Word Family list aloud
          several times.

Step 3.   Invent new words for the list. Print each new
          combination for your child to read. Remember,
          nonsense words can be used (*dat, kat, gat*).

Step 4.   Read the story *with* your child. He or she reads
          all of the Word Family words; you read the rest.

Step 5.   Have your child read the Sight Word list aloud
          several times.

Step 6.   Read the story *with* your child again. This time
          he or she reads the words from both lists; you
          read the rest.

Step 7.   Your child reads the entire book to you!

There are five sets of books in the

Series. Each set consists of five **FIRST BOOKS**
and two **BRING-IT-ALL-TOGETHER BOOKS**.

SET 1

is the first set your children should read.
The word families are selected from the short vowel sounds:
at, **ed**, **ish** and **im**, **op**, **ug**.

SET 2

provides more practice
with short vowel sounds:
an and **and**, **et**, **ip**, **og**, **ub**.

SET 3

focuses on
long vowel sounds:
ake, **eep**, **ide** and **ine**, **oke** and **ose**, **ue** and **ute**.

SET 4

introduces the idea that the word family sounds
can be spelled two different ways:
ale/ail, **een/ean**, **ight/ite**, **ote/oat**, **oon/une**.

SET 5

acquaints children with word families that
do not follow the rules for long and short vowel sounds:
all, **ound**, **y**, **ow**, **ew**.